the BAD GUYS

EPISODE

2

...SSION
...LUCKABLE

SCHOLASTIC CHILDREN'S BOOKS
AN IMPRINT OF SCHOLASTIC LTD
EUSTON HOUSE, 24 EVERSHOLT STREET, LONDON, NW1 1DB, UK
REGISTERED OFFICE: WESTFIELD ROAD, SOUTHAM, WARWICKSHIRE, CV47 0RA
SCHOLASTIC AND ASSOCIATED LOGOS ARE TRADEMARKS AND/OR REGISTERED TRADEMARKS
OF SCHOLASTIC INC.

FIRST PUBLISHED IN AUSTRALIA BY SCHOLASTIC AUSTRALIA, 2015
FIRST PUBLISHED IN THE UK BY SCHOLASTIC LTD, 2016

COPYRIGHT © AARON BLABEY, 2015

ISBN 978 1407 17057 2

A CIP CATALOGUE RECORD FOR THIS BOOK IS AVAILABLE FROM THE BRITISH LIBRARY.

PRINTED BY CPI GROUP (UK) LTD, CROYDON, CR0 4YY
PAPERS USED BY SCHOLASTIC CHILDREN'S BOOKS ARE MADE FROM WOOD GROWN IN
SUSTAINABLE FORESTS.

1 3 5 7 9 10 8 6 4 2

WWW.SCHOLASTIC.CO.UK

AARON BLABEY

the BAD GUYS

EPISODE 2

MISSION UNPLUCKABLE

SCHOLASTIC

NEWS FLASH!

PANIC AT THE DOG POUND!

We interrupt this program to bring you a breaking news story.

TIFFANY FLUFFIT is our reporter on the scene. Tiffany, what can you tell us?

CHUCK MELON

Thanks, Chuck!

Well, there have been **SHOCKING** scenes at the **DOG POUND** today.

It seems some kind of **CRAZED GANG** burst in, smashed down a wall and then drove away in a very loud hot-rod car, causing **200 TERRIFIED PUPPY DOGS** to run away in fright.

TIFFANY FLUFFIT 6

I have with me **MR GRAHAM PLONKER**,
Chief of Dog Pound Security.

Mr Plonker, how would you describe these
MONSTERS?

Ah . . . well . . . it all happened
so fast but . . . I'm pretty sure
there were four of them . . .

I mean, there was definitely a **WOLF**.

EXCLUSIVE FOOTAGE!

A really *mean*-looking wolf, with pointy teeth.

And there was a **SNAKE**.

HAVE YOU SEEN THIS SNAKE?

A very *ugly* snake, who also seemed quite cranky for some reason . . .

Ah, then there was a **YOUNG LADY** . . .

PRETTY GIRL? OR DEADLY SHARK?

. . . or possibly a gigantic **SHARK**. It was hard to tell which . . .

Oh yeah, and there was also some kind of nasty little fish.

MUTANT SARDINE ON THE LOOSE!

Maybe a **SARDINE**.

Not sure.

But Mr Plonker, would
you say that these
villains seemed . . .

DANGEROUS?

Oh yes, Tiffany. They're
dangerous, all right.

In fact, I'd say we are dealing
with some *serious* . . .

LIVE FROM THE DOG POUND

CHAPTER 1

OK, LET'S TRY THAT AGAIN

What's that guy talking about?
We **SAVED** those puppy dogs!
It was a
RESCUE!
We're the **GOOD GUYS** here!

AND FOR THE LAST TIME,
I AM **NOT** A SARDINE!
I'M A PIRANHA!

MUNCH! MUNCH! MUNCH!

See, Wolf? No-one is **EVER** going to believe we're good guys. I'm getting out of here before the cops come looking for us.

Oh, **NO** you don't, Mr Snake! We're not going to quit now. We're just getting started.

Don't forget **HOW GOOD** it felt to rescue those dogs!

All we need to do now is make sure that everyone can **SEE** that we're **HEROES**.

We just need to do something **SO AWESOME** that the whole world will sit up and take notice!

What did you have in mind, Mr Wolf?

THIS!

SUNNYSIDE
CHICKEN
FARM

You want us to break into a chicken farm?

Chickens?

Did you say . . . *chickens*?

A chicken farm? But that little chickie looks happy. She doesn't need to be rescued . . .

Oh, really?

Well, take a look INSIDE
Sunnyside Chicken Farm, fellas.

10,000 CHICKENS!

Stuffed into **TINY** cages!

24 hours a day!

With **NO** sunlight!

And **NO** room to run and play!

But that's awful!
That's the worst thing
I've ever heard!

What are we waiting for?!

WE NEED TO SET THOSE
LITTLE CHICKIE-BABIES
FREE!

Let's go! Let's go! Let's go!
Let's go! Let's go! Let's go!
Let's go! Let's go! Let's go!
Let's go! Let's go! Let's go!
LET'S GO!

Well, *hellooooo . . .*

Are you OK, man?

Huh?

DROOL

Oh yeah . . . sorry.
I was just thinking that chickens are delicious—I mean, *DELIGHTFUL*— and I think we need to save them all **RIGHT NOW**.

Oh, if only it were that simple, my friend. But I'm afraid I have some bad news . . .

Sunnyside Chicken Farm is

IMPOSSIBLE

to break into!

It's a **MAXIMUM SECURITY CHICKEN FARM** with **STEEL WALLS** that are 30 feet high and 8 feet thick!

There are **NO WINDOWS** and all the doors are **HEAVILY GUARDED.**

SUNNYSIDE
INC

And even if you *did* get inside, you'd be caught instantly because . . .

If you touch the FLOOR, an **ALARM** goes off!

If you touch the WALLS, an **ALARM** goes off!

And if you walk into the LASER BEAMS, an **ALARM** goes off!

• FLOOR ALARMS

• WALL ALARMS

• LASER ALARMS

Did you say
LASER BEAMS?
Why are you even showing us this, chico? We don't have the skills to pull off a job like this!

No, we don't.
But I know a guy who does.

Who?

• CHAPTER 2 •
the
FREAKY GEEK

Hey, dudes! It's totally
awesome to meet you!

Aieeeeee!
RUN CHICOS! It's a
TARANTULA!!!

I'm sorry about this, Legs.
I don't know what's
wrong with them.

Aw, it's cool.
Happens all the time.

LEGS?!

You *know* this monster?!

What were you thinking,
bringing a tarantula into
our clubhouse?

. . . Can't breathe . . .
spider . . .
Mummy . . .
Mummy . . .
I want my mummy . . .

Mr Shark! Pull yourself together!
You guys should be ASHAMED of yourselves!
LEGS is just like us.
He's a GOOD GUY with a BAD reputation.

Aw, thanks,
Wolfie.

He's **DANGEROUS,** man.

Yeah!
And why isn't he
wearing any pants?

I don't do pants, dude. I like to feel free.

. . . can't breathe . . .
no pants . . .
freaking . . . out . . .

Okey doke.

Legs? Why don't you
show them what you can do?

OK. Let's start with something simple.

TAP! TAP! TAP! TAP! TAP! TAP! TAP!

ACCESS: GRANTED
Name: MR SNAKE
Status: Very Dangerous
Action: Do Not Approach

HIGHEST SECURITY

Hey! That's my police file!

Geez, they don't like you very much, do they?

But **NOBODY** can access that! There's no way you can hack into their system. That's the toughest security there is!

Yeah, it *is* kind of tricky.

TAP! TAP! TAP! TAP! TAP! TAP! TAP!

But it's worth it just to see you smile, Mr Snake.

Ta-da!

That's
IMPOSSIBLE!

Not for a **SUPERHACKER** like Legs! He's a computer **GENIUS**. And he has a plan that will get us inside that chicken farm.

Thanks, Wolfie. But first, I'd better put this back the way I found it. We are good guys, after all . . .

. . . and I wouldn't like to get us in trouble. Sorry, Mr Snake. You're *dangerous* again, I'm afraid.

Hey!

This is **SO** cool, guys! I'm so happy to be part of the team. And I bet by this time tomorrow, we're totally going to be **BESTIES!**

. . . *spider* . . .

. . . *with no pants* . . .

. . . *on my head* . . .

Hey, chico. I got one word for you— *trousers.*

· CHAPTER 3 ·

MISSION, LIKE, TOTALLY IMPOSSIBLE

OK, dudes, I took your advice and found myself some clothes. What do you think?

I can still see his
BIG FURRY BUTT.

Cut it out,
Piranha.
Just listen
to him.

OK.

To get you guys inside
Sunnyside Chicken Farm,
all I need to do is hack into
their main computer and
switch off all the alarms.

BUT

there's a problem . . .

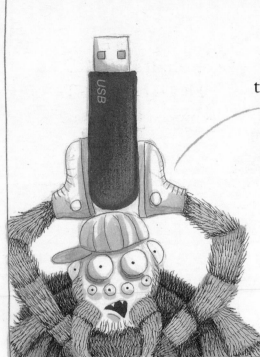

The security is
SO HIGH
that I can't do it from here.

I need you guys to plug
THIS THING
into their computer,
so I can access it.

Once you do that, I can
SHUT IT ALL DOWN
and get you to those
chickens.

Wait a minute. You're telling
us that you can hack into my
police file, but you **CAN'T**
get into a CHICKEN FARM
without our help?

Yeah. It's WEIRD. This is one SCARY chicken farm, dude.

But if it's so scary, how do we get to the computer? Wolf said there's no way into the building!

Well, there is **ONE** way.

But it sure isn't easy . . .

There's a **SMALL HATCH** on the roof.

You'll need to go through the hatch and **DROP** 30 metres on a rope to the computer below. Once you get to it, **JUST PLUG ME IN**.

BUT!

If you touch the WALLS or the FLOOR, the **ALARMS** will go off and you'll get caught.

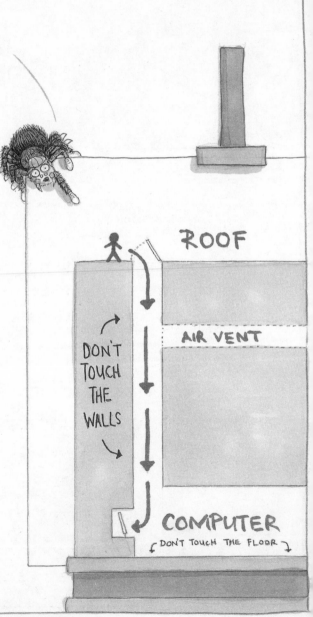

ROOF

DON'T TOUCH THE WALLS

AIR VENT

COMPUTER

(DON'T TOUCH THE FLOOR)

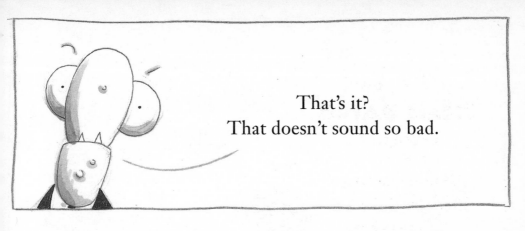

That's it?
That doesn't sound so bad.

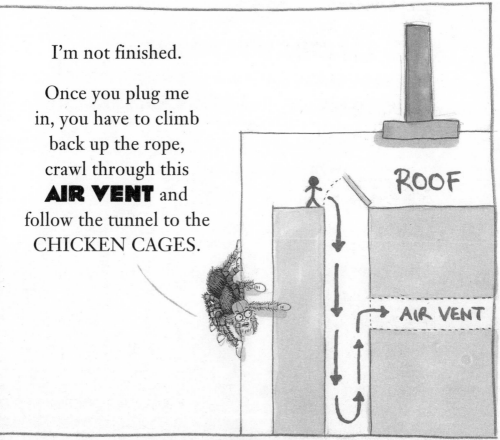

I'm not finished.

Once you plug me in, you have to climb back up the rope, crawl through this **AIR VENT** and follow the tunnel to the CHICKEN CAGES.

ROOF

AIR VENT

Like I said, that doesn't
sound so bad.

I'M STILL NOT FINISHED.

You see, before you reach the chicken cages,
you'll come to the **LASER BEAMS**.
And if you touch one, the alarms will go off.

Oh, and they'll zap you.
And they *really* hurt.

AIR VENT

LASERS

But why are the lasers still on?
I thought you were going to shut
down all the alarms?

I will.
The **OTHER** alarms will be off.

But the **LASER ALARMS**
can only be turned off by hand.
You have to flick a switch
once you're inside.

So . . . we just switch them off?

Yep.

That *still* doesn't sound so bad.

That's because I'm **STILL NOT FINISHED!**

The switch is on the OTHER SIDE of the laser beams, so you have to GO **THROUGH** THEM to reach it!

CHICKENS THIS WAY

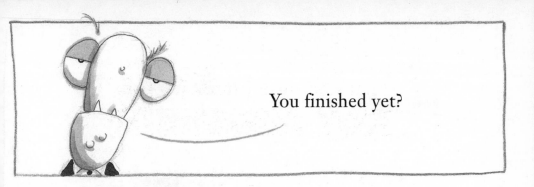

You finished yet?

Ahhh . . . yep.

Good! Because
that sounds

LOCO!

There's **NO WAY** we
can pull this off, man!

Oh yes, we can!

But **ONLY** if we work as a **TEAM!**

So, Snake and Piranha—

you guys are coming with ME!

We are going to **GET INSIDE**,

plug **THIS THING** into the computer and

GET TO THOSE CHICKENS!

This is going to be

GREAT!

But . . . what about me?

You're going to be working with me, Big Guy.
It's OUR JOB to get these guys in and out of there safely!
Isn't this awesome? You and I are going to SPEND A
LOT OF TIME TOGETHER!

Oh . . . that's . . .
great . . . but . . .
I think . . .
I'm going . . .
to cry . . .

No time for tears, Mr Shark.

WE'VE GOT CHICKENS TO SAVE!

• CHAPTER 4 •
DOWN THE HATCH

Hey, what are you guys
doing all the way over there?

LATER THAT NIGHT . . .

SUNNYSIDE
CHICKEN FARM
KEEP OUT!

We look ridiculous.

SUNNYSIDE
INC

Hey, Tarantula! What's with the stupid suits?

Shhh! Not so loud, Mr Piranha. These suits are GREAT! They'll keep you cool and make you really hard to spot.

PLUS!

Each suit has a microphone and earpiece, so we can all talk to each other.

GOT IT?

Hey, Wolf, do you really promise there'll be chickens down there?

It's a **CHICKEN** FARM! Of course there'll be chickens. Why are you so worried about that?

Oh, no reason.

I just really **LOVE** chickens, man.

They're so nice to eat—
I mean, they're so nice to *MEET*.

Yeah . . .

You DO understand that we're here to SAVE the chickens, don't you?

Uh-huh.

And you wouldn't try to **EAT** any chickens, would you?

Uh-uh.

Hey! Can we just DO THIS? My jumpsuit is chafing.

OK. OK. OK. Well, the walls are a *little* closer than I'd expected.

Mr Shark! Whatever you do, make sure you lower us *SLOWLY*.

I hear you.

BOING!

Do you need a hand, Big Buddy?

EEEEEEEEE

FOOF!

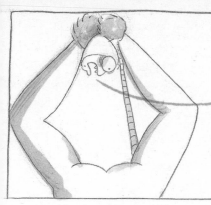

Whoa. That was close.

¡AY, CARAMBA!

Mr Wolf?
Has anyone ever told you that your
face looks like a **BUTT?**

What?

Oh. Sorry. My mistake.

Hey, look! The computer!
I think I can reach it . . .

He didn't see us.
Why didn't he see us?

Are you kidding?
WE GET
OUT OF
HERE!
SHARK?!
ABORT!
ABORT!
PULL US
UP NOW!

Shhh! I don't know.
He must have really bad eyesight.
Um . . . OK . . .
Any suggestions on what we do now?

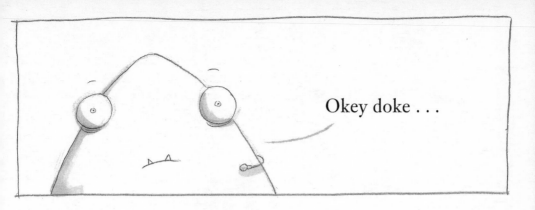

Okey doke . . .

NO! WAIT!

Look what he's eating, chicos.
That's a sardine sandwich.

I think I have an idea.

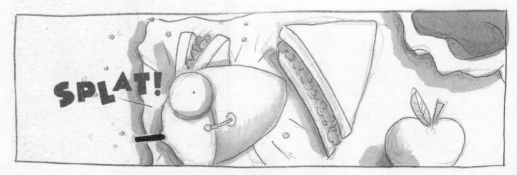

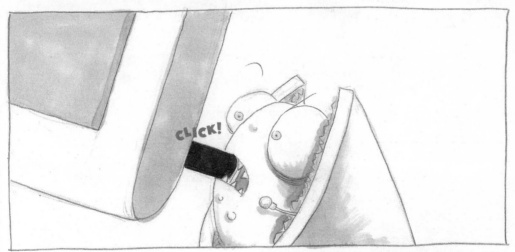

This was a one-way ticket, chico.

WHAT? We can't just leave you behind!

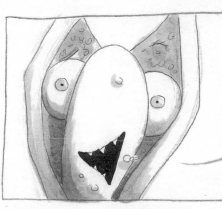

You have to, hermanos.
There is no other way.

Go and save those little
chickens, man.
Save them for **ME!**

Wolf! Snap out of it!
SHARK! Pull us up!

You got it.

Hurry up, man.
Just get in the vent, will you?

Look at him down there!

What a brave little guy!

He sacrificed himself for us.

Adios, chicos.

Yeah, yeah. Let's do this. I'm starving—I mean, I'm *STARTING* to want to save some chickens. Yep.

You're right. We should go.

Adios, Mr Piranha.

Stay safe.

Easy for you to say, baby.

· CHAPTER 5 ·
MIND THE GAP

See, Mr Snake? This is what I've been talking about— without Mr Piranha, we would **NEVER** have made it this far. **THAT'S** what being in a team is all about. **CO-OPERATION.**

Yeah, yeah, yeah, that's *so* interesting, but WHERE ARE THE CHICKENS, man?

Just up ahead, I'd say.

This bit has been a lot easier than I thought. I really don't know what all the fuss was ab—

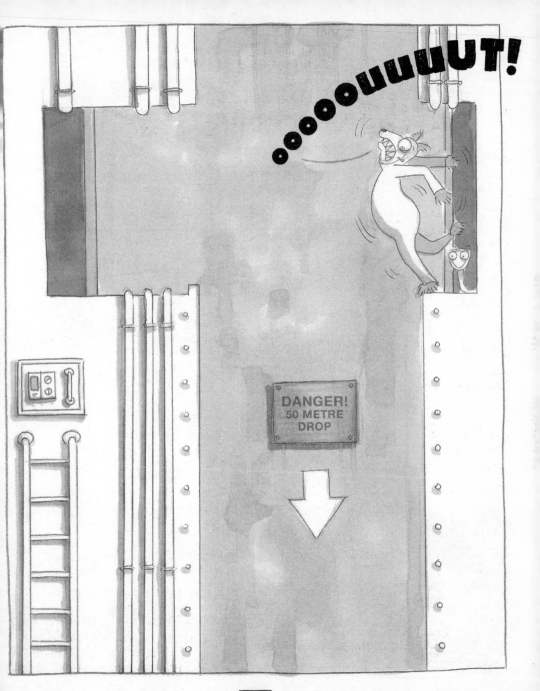

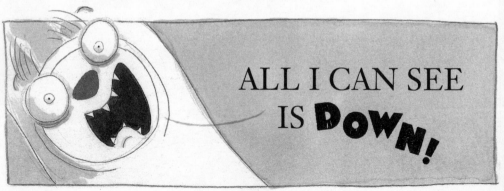

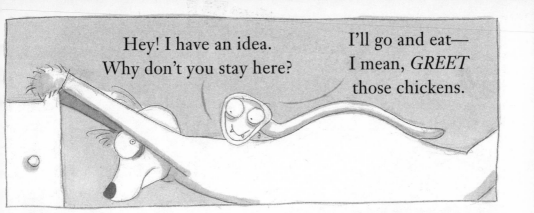

Hey! I have an idea.
Why don't you stay here?

I'll go and eat—
I mean, *GREET*
those chickens.

Noooo! I'm slipping!
I . . . can't hold on.
You have to . . . help me . . .

Really?
That's a bit annoying.

ANNOYING?!
IF YOU DON'T HELP ME,
I'M GOING TO **DIE!**

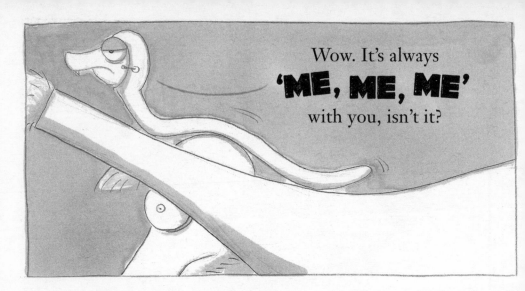

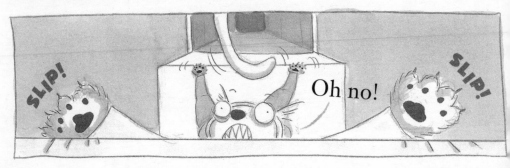

BETTER?!

How is this 'better'?

DANGER!
50 METRE
DROP

You need to go
on a diet, man.
You really do.

Now, let's think.

What do we do?

We're trapped.

It's not just ME
that's trapped. And
it's not just YOU.
It's **US**.

We're trapped as
a **TEAM**. So we
need to get out of
this as a **TEAM**.

I'VE **GOT** IT!

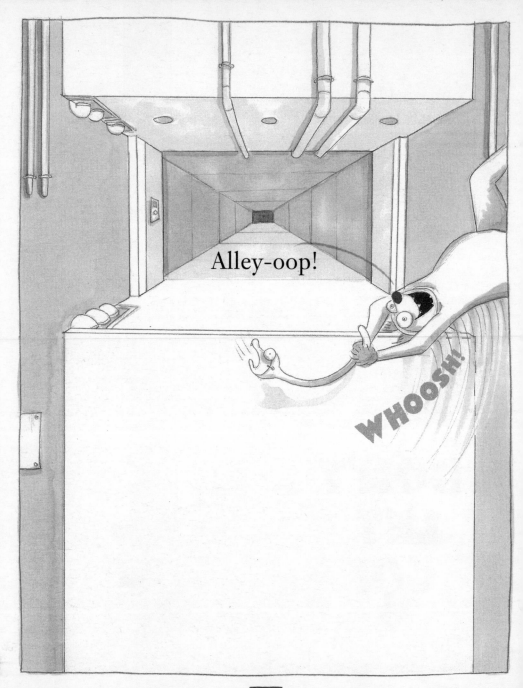

· CHAPTER 6 ·
LET'S START OVER

That's not good.

Piranha?
Can you hear me?

Mr Shark? Is that you?

I'm about to be a monkey's lunch here, man.

You sit tight, Mr P.
I'm coming to get you.

BOING!

Can I help,
BIG
FELLA?

ARRRRGGGGHHH!

PLEASE don't . . .
can't breathe . . .
please don't . . .
really please don't . . .
can't breathe . . .

Hey, what's your problem, dude?

Really . . . scared . . . of . . . spiders . . .

Uh-huh. And why is that?
It's OK, you can tell me.

OK, well . . .

you're **FREAKY** to look at because
you have **TOO MANY EYES** and

TOO MANY LEGS

and I'm SO creeped
out by you that

**I MIGHT
THROW UP!**

But . . . I'm sorry if that
sounds rude.

It's OK.

No, really. I feel terrible saying
that. You must think I'm awful.

No, that's OK.
You seem like a nice guy.
But can I ask you one little thing?

Yes, of course.

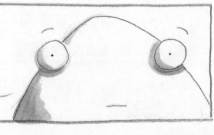

Well . . .

since I can't help being a tarantula in the same way

that you CAN'T HELP BEING A

MASSIVE, TERRIFYING SEA MONSTER,

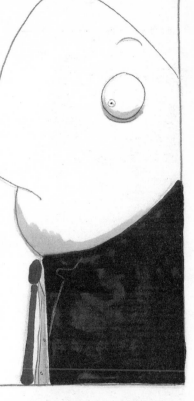

I wonder
if you could just

GET OVER IT

and then

MAYBE

I could help you rescue
your friend!

Um . . . OK.

I'm so sorry. That was really uncool.

It's OK. That's good advice.

Well . . . um . . . how are we going to rescue that piranha?

I've heard you're pretty good at disguises. Is that right?

I have my moments.

OK, well, I'm REALLY good at making stuff. So why don't we work together?

OK.

But what kind of disguise is going to get me inside a chicken farm?

Why don't you pull the feathers out of those pillows there, Mr Shark, and I'll tell you my idea.

CHAPTER 7

TRUST ME, I'M A SNAKE

Oh no! Look at those laser beams! I'll **NEVER** get through!

I think we have a problem.

CAGE ➡

Oooooh no, no, no, no. There's no problem—I'll fit through those lasers. I'll just have to handle this one **ALONE.**

Are you sure?

Oh, ABSOLUTELY.
I'll just wriggle my way across and have a chicken feast—I mean . . . I'll get those chickens **RELEASED.**

Yeah.
Released.
Heh heh.

But you'll switch off the lasers when you get across?

Yeah, yeah, sure.

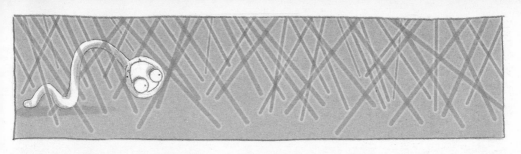

YOU **MADE** IT!

You're amazing!

Now, just switch off the
lasers so I can get across . . .

Hmmm, sure.

Just give me a few minutes
to find the switch . . .

You take your time, little buddy!

YOU ROCK!

I'm just SO proud of these guys.

WHISTLE
WHISTLE

Geez, it's been fifteen minutes.

Are you OK over there, Mr Snake?

Aha! He's done it.

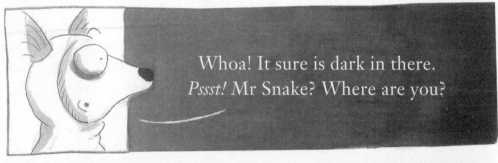

Whoa! It sure is dark in there.
Pssst! Mr Snake? Where are you?

Oh, there you are!
Is everything OK?

Urghugh.

Mr Snake?

What are you doing
over there?

In the dark?

Behind all those . . .
EMPTY cages?

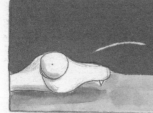

Gnnughgagh.

You sound funny, man.
Are you OK?

Sgllurrr!

Oh no.

Wait a minute—
You didn't—

SNAKE?!
WHAT DID
YOU DO?!!

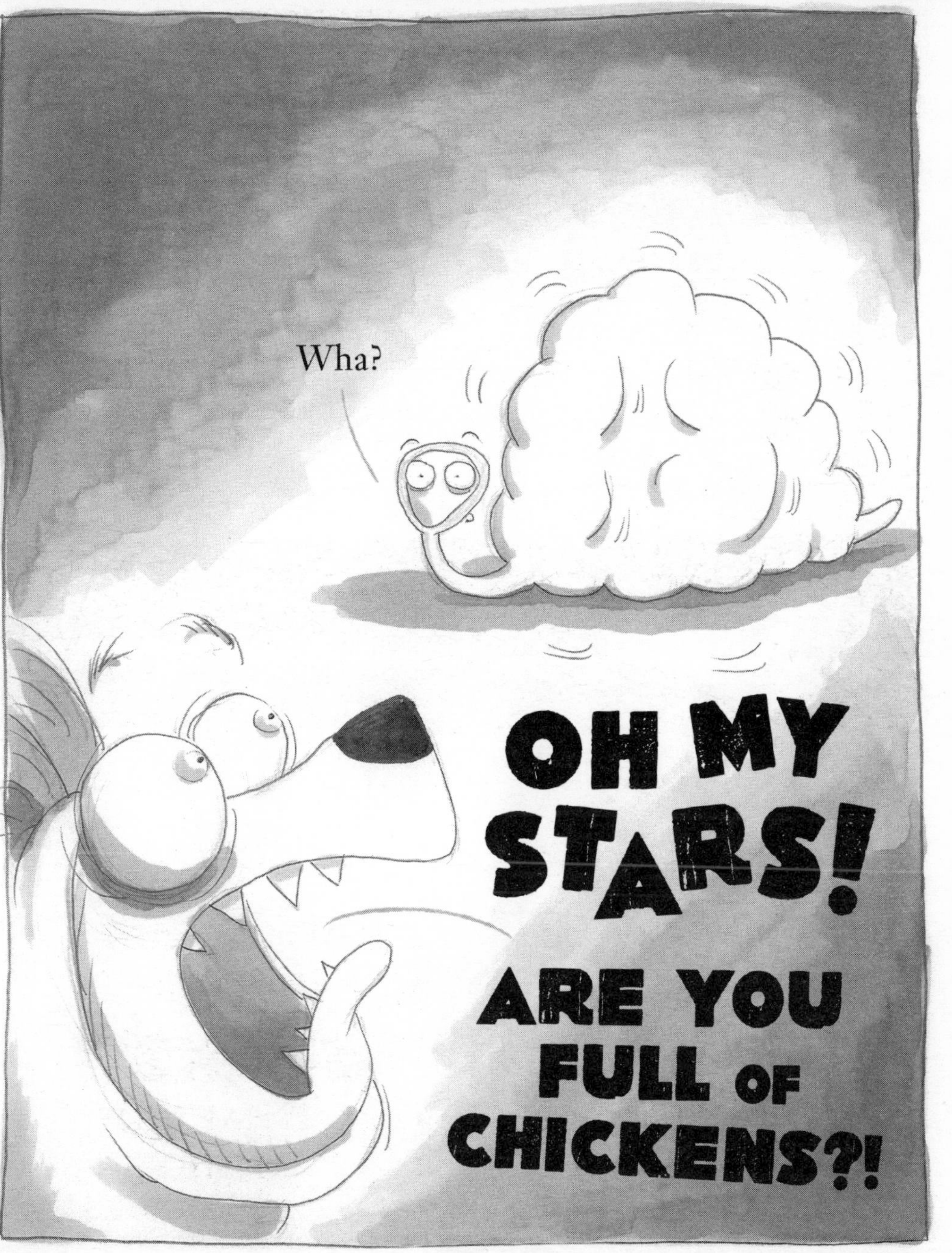
Wha?
OH MY STARS!
ARE YOU FULL OF CHICKENS?!

Oh, I don't think so.

Snake, you are *not* going to ruin this plan. No, you are not.

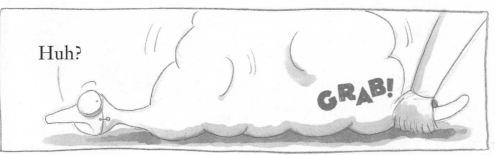

Huh?

GRAB!

NO.
YOU.
ARE.
NOT.

· CHAPTER 8 ·
WHOLE LOTTA CHICKEN

¡Ay Caramba!

This is the end, amigos!

Hey, Clive! One of the chickens escaped, but we've managed to catch it again.

What?

Who knows? But let's get it back down to the cages.

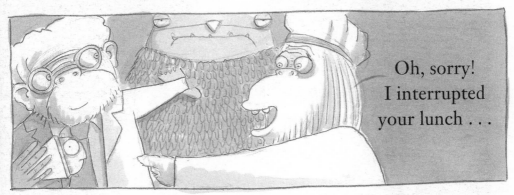

Oh, sorry! I interrupted your lunch . . .

Aw, that's OK. I can eat on the run.

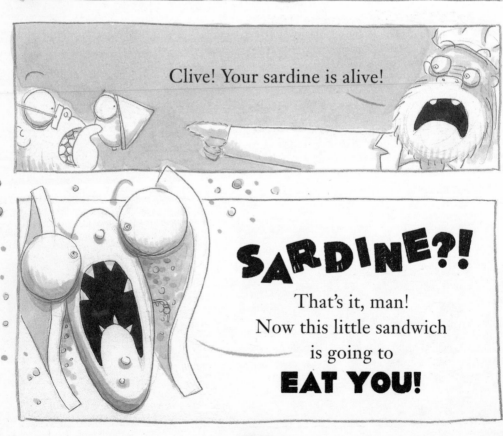

ARRGGHHH!!!

Yeah, I'm your **WORST** nightmare, hombre! I'm a piranha burger with **EXTRA SPICE!**

Mr Shark? Is that you?

Yep.

Wow! I barely recognised you.

Yeah, I know.
I'm good at disguises.

WHOOP! WHOOP! WHOOP!

OH NO! They've set off the alarm!

WHOOP! WHOOP! WHOOP!

But Wolf and Snake will be trapped!

Guys! It's Legs! Get out of there! They're coming for you!

WHOOP! WHOOP! WHOOP!

We're not leaving without our chicos.

Or our chickens.

WHOOP! WHOOP!

The alarm!
We have to hurry!

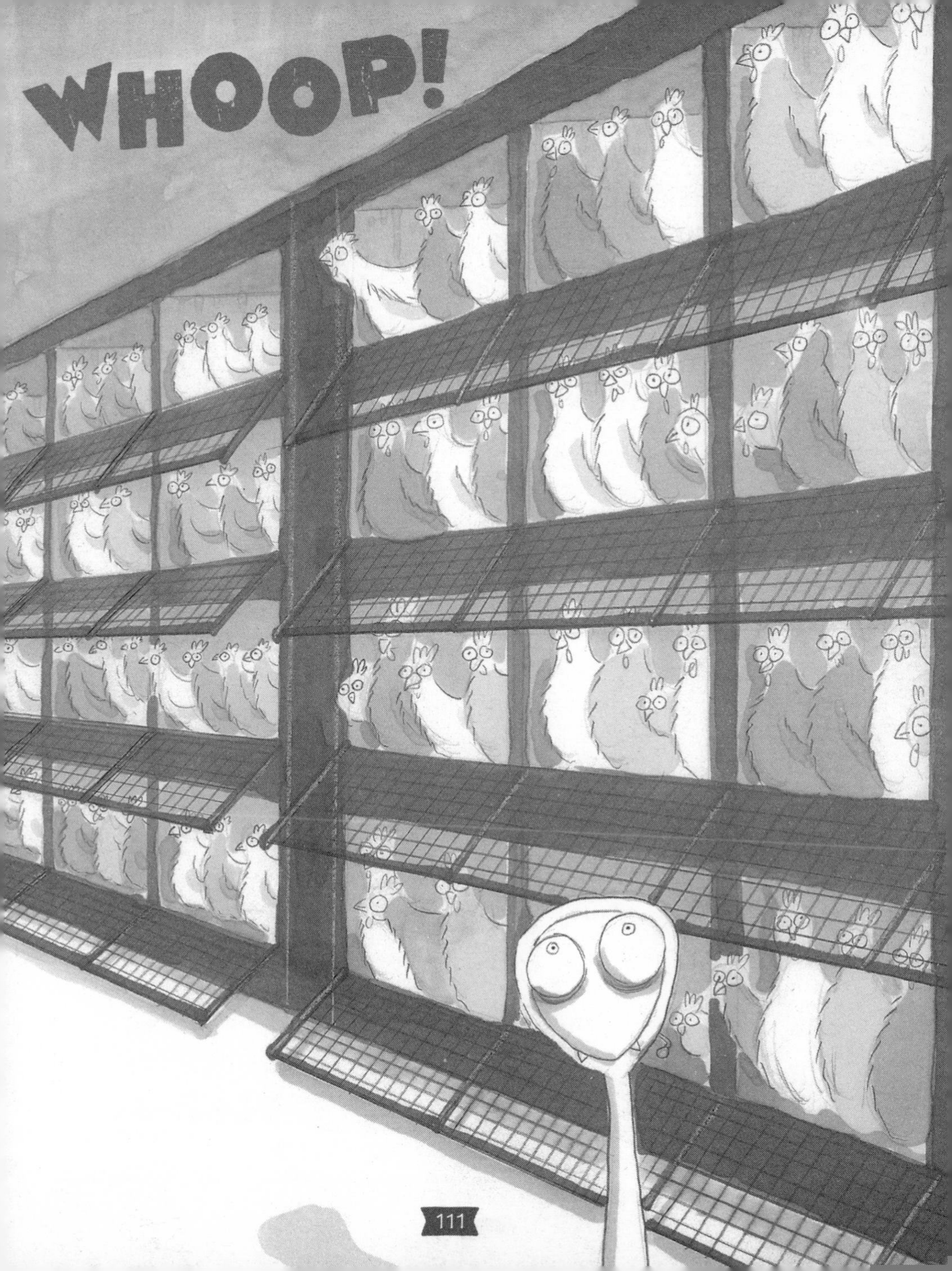
WHOOP!

We've opened the cages, but they won't run. What's wrong with these stupid chickens?

They're scared.

Of what?

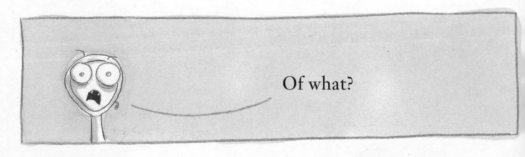

OF THE CREEP WHO TRIED TO **EAT THEM!**

I couldn't help it.

I'm sorry.

Yeah, well, 'sorry' won't help
us now, Mr Snake.

What are we going to do?
The chickens are terrified.

They need someone to
FOLLOW.

They need someone to **TRUST**.

They need . . .

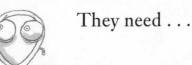

Wow. That's one big chicken.

All right, girls. I know you're scared, but this is your **ONE CHANCE** to get out of this horrible place.

Do you understand?

GOOD.

Run, little chickies! Run!

THEN LET'S GET OUT OF HERE!

Mr Piranha!
You're here!

Are you OK?

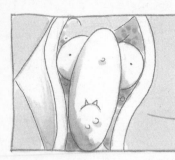

I'm completely coated
in mayonnaise.

Oh. I see.

It's not too bad, actually.

I kind of like it.

Throw me at him!
It's your only chance!

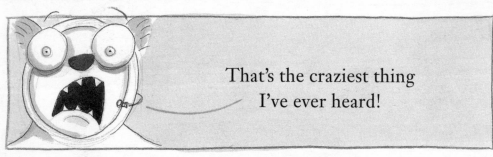

That's the craziest thing
I've ever heard!

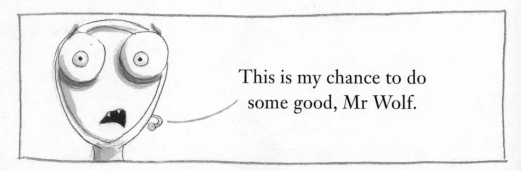

This is my chance to do
some good, Mr Wolf.

But—

THROW ME NOW OR THESE CHICKENS WILL NEVER BE FREE! **DO IT!**

And don't miss.
GOT IT?

Got it.

Hi. Let's play a game. The first person to open the door doesn't get bitten by a snake.

You win.

Now, can I ask you to please lock all the guards in behind us after we leave?

Oh, and if you don't, I **WILL** find out where you live and you **WILL** find me in your bed in the middle of the night.

Do we have a deal?

Yes, we do.

Marvellous!

BOING!

See? You're not the only Good Guy around here . . .

I knew it! I knew it! I knew it!

OK. Less hugs. More escaping.

· CHAPTER 9 ·
WHAT A TEAM

I am so proud of you guys!
10,000 chickens are free
because of **YOU!**

I think we're starting to get the hang of this hero thing, fellas.

And that means you, too, Mr Snake.

OK, Huggy Bear. Let's not make a great big hairy deal out of it.

Aw, sure thing, you old grouch! Let's get out of here . . .

But . . .

What happened to the **CAR?!**

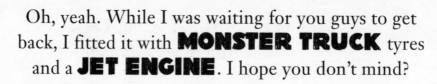

Oh, yeah. While I was waiting for you guys to get back, I fitted it with **MONSTER TRUCK** tyres and a **JET ENGINE**. I hope you don't mind?

We don't mind!

And I noticed that you seemed a little cramped in there, Mr Shark, so I've modified your seat. If you don't like it, I can always put it back the way it was.

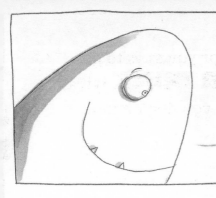

I . . . I *love* it, Legs.
You're very thoughtful.

Thank you.

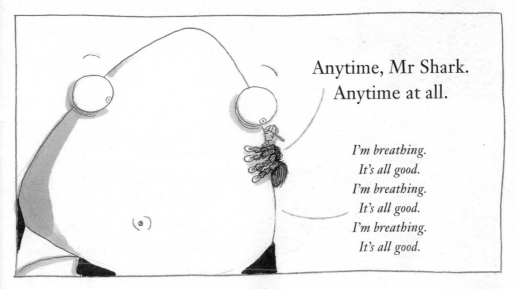

Anytime, Mr Shark.
Anytime at all.

I'm breathing.
It's all good.
I'm breathing.
It's all good.
I'm breathing.
It's all good.

SQUEAK!

Hey! Did
anybody else
hear that?

Hmmm.
It seems to be coming from that

CREEPY OLD HOUSE

next to the chicken farm that we . . .
somehow didn't notice. Perhaps it's
a chicken that's lost its way?

I didn't know chickens
could squeak . . .

Nope. My mistake.
There's nothing here. It's empty.

Well, no. It's not
completely empty . . .

Look!

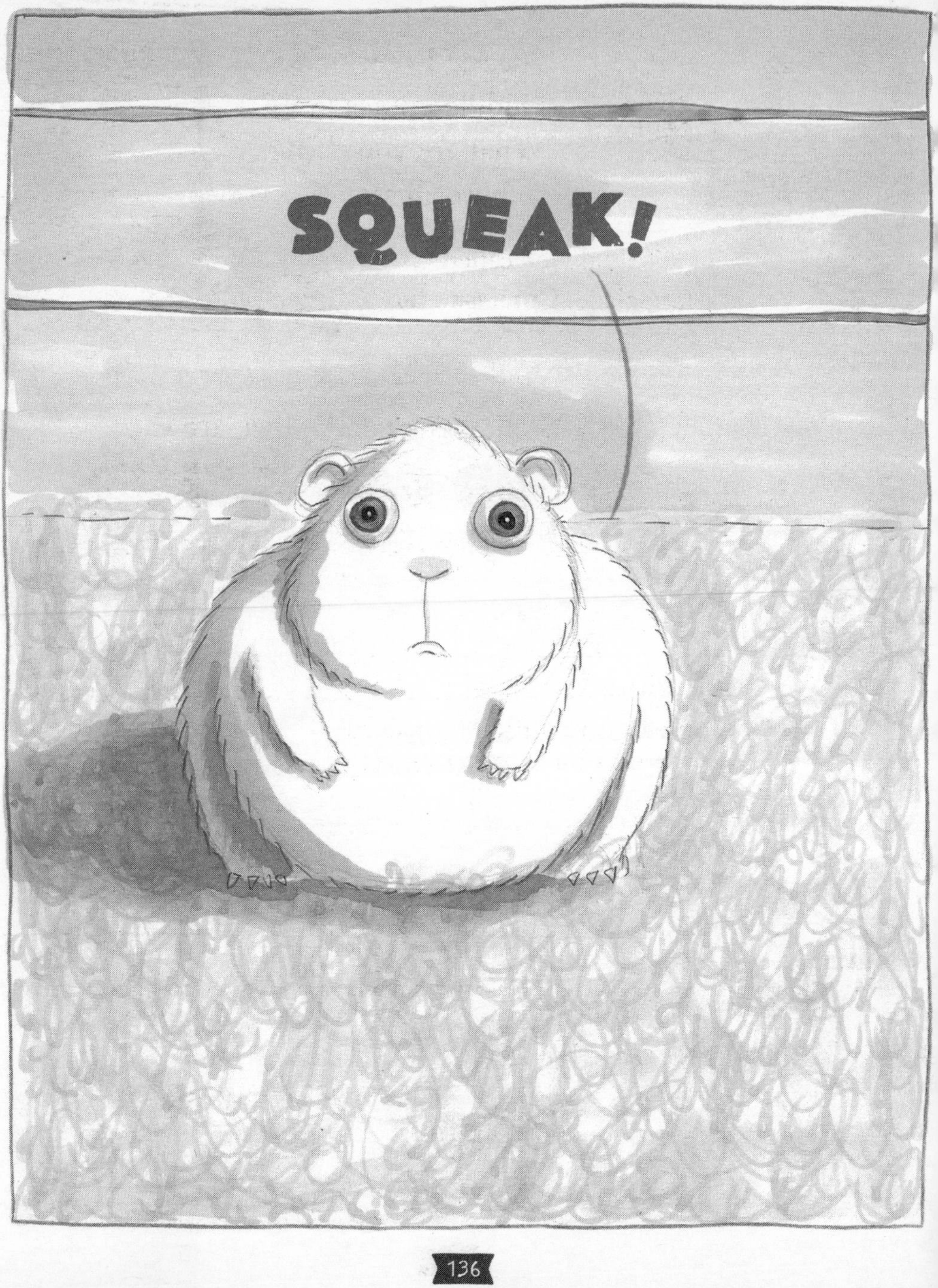
SQUEAK!

Awww! Look at the widdle guinea pig! What are you doing here all alone?

I think he's called Marmalade. Cute, isn't he?

Well, Marmalade—we are the

GOOD GUYS CLUB.

And we have come to set you free!

You take care, little Marmalade.
ENJOY YOUR FREEDOM!

See you, little guy.

Good . . . guys?

GOOD GUYS?

And just because they call themselves
GOOD GUYS, they think they can

BREAK INTO MY CHICKEN FARM AND SET MY CHICKENS FREE?!

AND THEY THINK THEY CAN
GET AWAY WITH IT?

Well, we'll see about that. I shall make them pay.

Oh, yes . . .

Boy, did these guys mess with the

WRONG

guinea pig!

See what happens when the Bad Guys get captured by a **REALLY bad guy.**

How will they escape from his evil lair? **Who** is that mysterious **NINJA** that seems to be following them? And **when** will they all stop trying to **EAT** each other?!

Don't miss their next **so-funny-you'll-wet-your-pants** adventure—

the BAD GUYS

EPISODE

COMING SOON!

The Bad Guys are about to have a *really* BAD day . . .